This book belongs to

....

Published by Ladybird Books Ltd
A Penguin Company
Penguin Books Ltd, 80 Strand, London WC2R 0RL, UK
Penguin Books Australia Ltd, Camberwell, Victoria, Australia
Penguin Group (NZ) 67 Apollo Drive, Rosedale, North Shore 0632, New Zealand

002 – 10 9 8 7 6 5 4 3 2

© Ladybird Books Ltd MCMXCIX
This edition MMXI

ISBN: 978-1-40931-133-1

Printed in China

Ladybird First Favourite Tales

The Gingerbread Man

BASED ON A TRADITIONAL FOLK TALE
retold by Alan MacDonald ★ illustrated by Anja Rieger

One morning a baker said to his wife,
"Today I'll bake a gingerbread man.
He'll look just right in our shop window."

So the baker made a gingerbread man and put him in the oven. Before long they heard a noise. A little voice began to shout,

"Open the door! Let me out!"

The baker and his wife chased him down
the street, shouting, "Come back here,
little ginger feet!"

But the gingerbread man just ran and
ran, singing,

…a hungry boy joined the chase, calling, "Come back here, little ginger face!"

But the gingerbread man just ran and ran, singing,

…a hungry cow who said,
"Come back here, little ginger head!"

But the gingerbread man just ran and
ran, singing,

"Run, run as fast as you ca

…a hungry horse, neighing,
"Come back here, little ginger paws!"

But the gingerbread man just ran and
ran, singing,

Hey! Neigh!

"Run, run, as fast as you can,
You can't catch me, I'm the gingerbread man"

Behind him chased the horse, the cow, the boy, the baker and his wife.

In the woods hid a hungry fox. He called, "What's the hurry, little ginger socks?"

But the gingerbread man just ran and ran, singing,

He was just thinking how clever he was, when…

…he came to a wide, wide river.

The gingerbread man stopped. He needed to think. Up crept the fox and said with a wink,

"Jump onto my tail and I'll take you across."

The gingerbread man thanked the sly fox and he jumped onto his bushy tail.

The fox started to swim across the wide, wide river.

Very soon he said, "Little gingerbread man, you're too heavy for my tail. Why not jump onto my red, red back?"

So the gingerbread man jumped onto the fox's back.

But soon the fox said, "Little gingerbread man, you're too heavy for my back. Why not hop onto my shiny, black nose?"

So the gingerbread man hopped
onto the fox's nose.

Just as they came near to the bank, the fox tossed back his head.

And with a flick of his neck, he tossed the gingerbread man up, up, up in the air.

Then the gingerbread man fell

down, down, down...

SNAP! straight into the fox's gaping mouth.

And that was the end of the gingerbread man.

With a sly smile, the fox trotted home, singing,

*"Run, run, as fast as you can,
But I caught **you**, little gingerbread man!"*